MW01144973

Dropping In On...

PUERTO RICO

Patricia M. Moritz

A Geography Series

ROURKE CORPORATION, INC.
VERO BEACH, FLORIDA 32964

Printed in the United States of America.

Library of Congress Cataloging-In-Publication Data

Moritz, Patricia M.
Puerto Rico/Patricia M. Moritz.
p. cm. — (Dropping in on)
Includes index.
Summary: Describes some of the major cities and regions of the Caribbean island of Puerto Rico, a commonwealth of the United States.
ISBN 0-86593-492-4
1. Puerto Rico—Description and travel—Juvenile literature.
[1. Puerto Rico—Description and travel.] I. Title.
II. Series.
F1965.3.M67 1998
917.29504'52—dc21 98-15473
CIP
AC

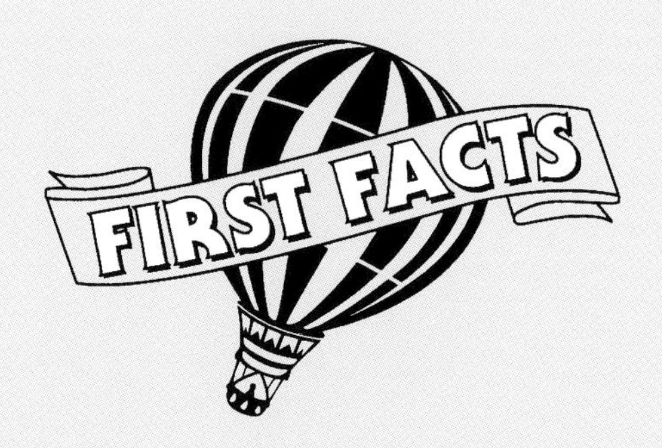

Puerto Rico

Official Name:
Commonwealth of Puerto Rico

Area: 3,435 square miles
(8,897 square kilometers)

Population: 3.5 million

Capital: San Juan

Largest City: San Juan (pop. 437,750)

Highest Elevation:
Cerro de Punta, 4,390 feet (1,338 meters)

Official Language: Spanish

Major Religions: Roman Catholic (80%)
other Christian (20%)

Money: U.S. dollar

Form of Government: Self-governing commonwealth of the United States

Flag:

TABLE OF CONTENTS

Our Blue Ball—The Earth

The Earth can be divided into two hemispheres. The word hemisphere means "half a ball"—in this case, the ball is the Earth.

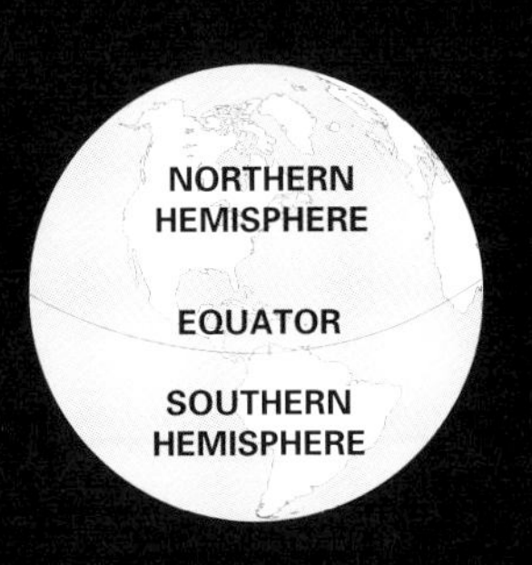

The equator is an imaginary line that runs around the middle of the Earth. It separates the Northern Hemisphere from the Southern Hemisphere. North America—where Canada, the United States, and Mexico are located—is in the Northern Hemisphere.

The Northern Hemisphere

When the North Pole is tilted toward the sun, the sun's most powerful rays strike the northern half of the Earth and less sunshine hits the Southern Hemisphere. That is when people in the Northern Hemisphere enjoy summer. When the

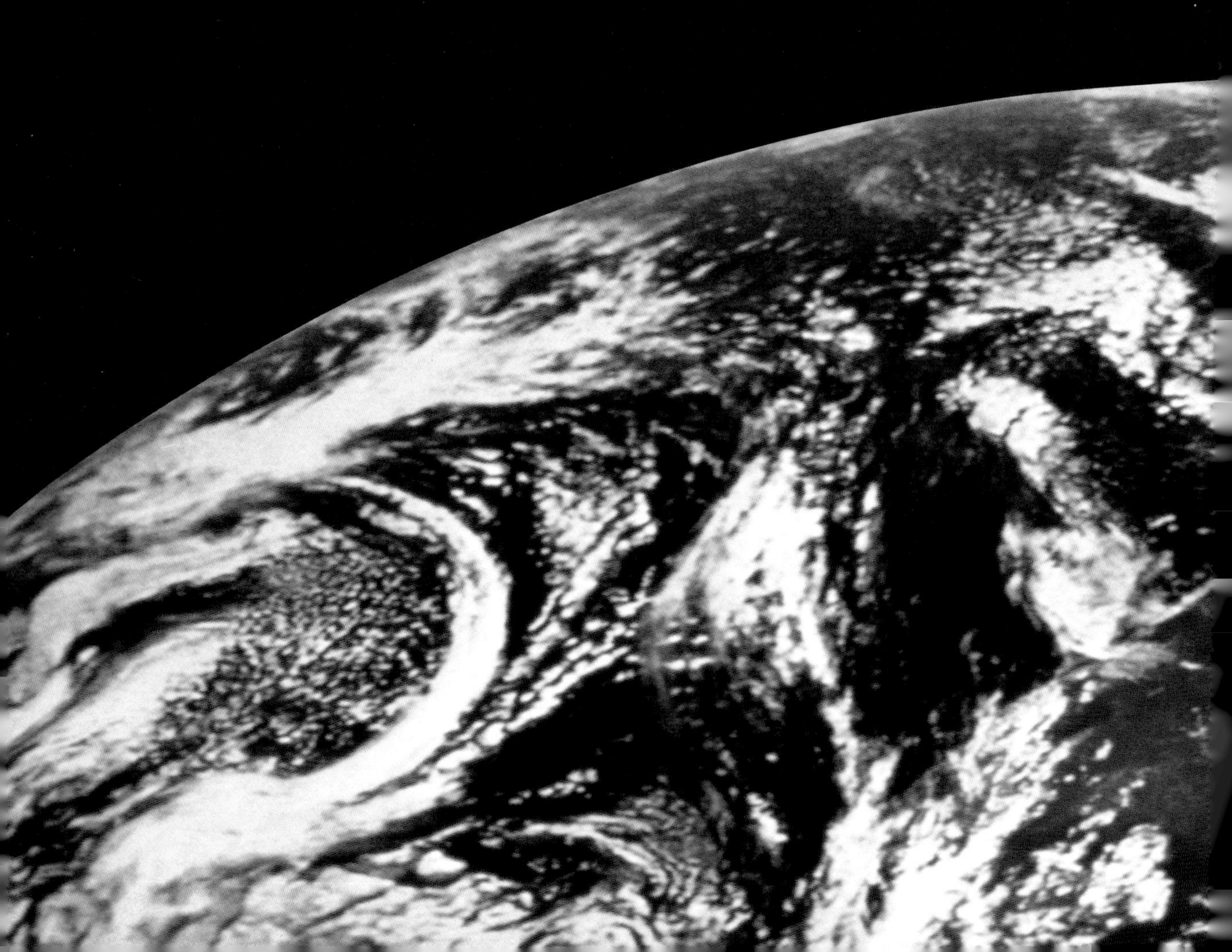

North Pole is tilted away from the sun, and the Southern Hemisphere receives the most sunshine, the seasons reverse. Then winter comes to the Northern Hemisphere. Seasons in the Northern Hemisphere and the Southern Hemisphere are always opposite.

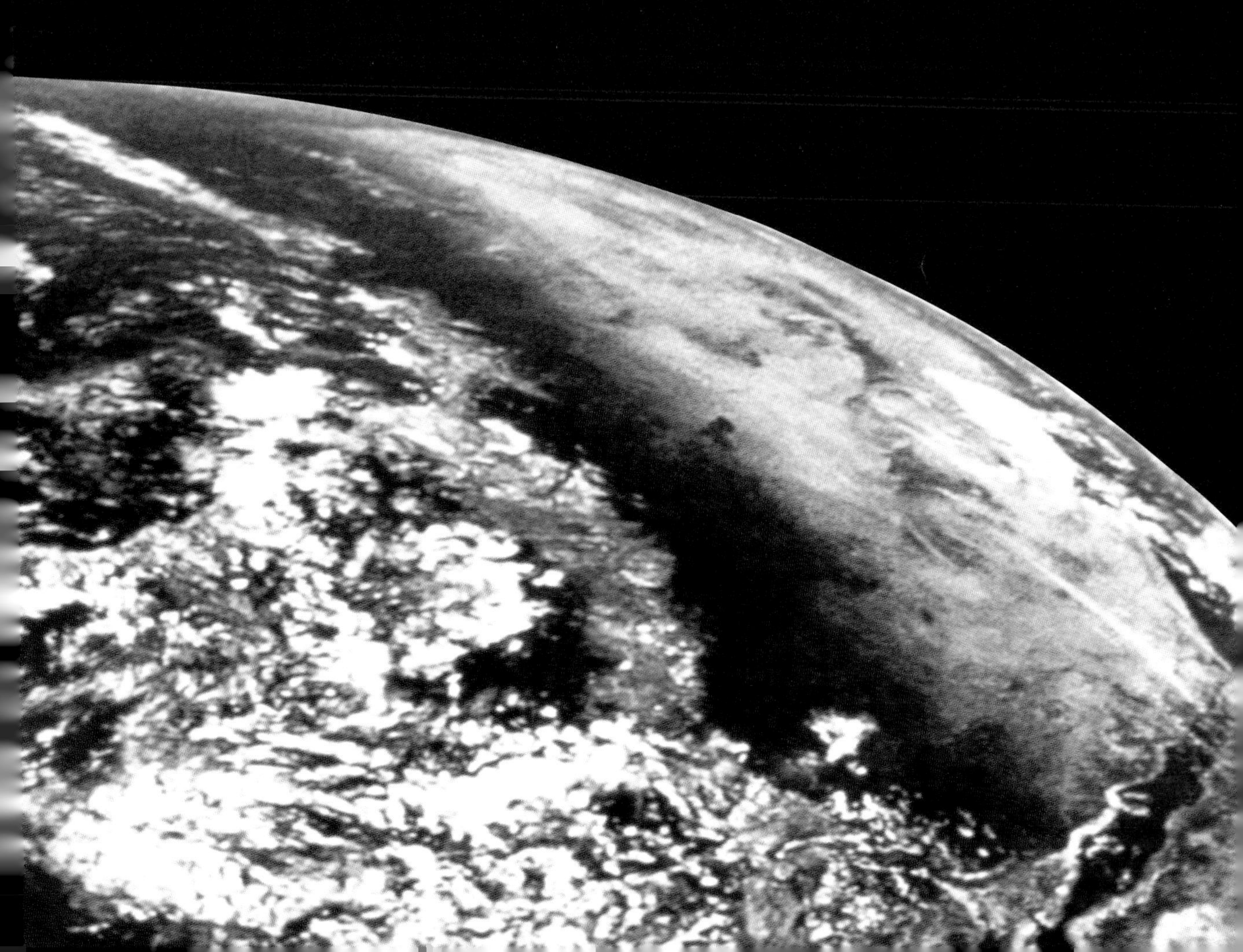

Get Ready for Puerto Rico

Let's take a trip! Climb into your hot-air balloon, and we'll drop in on a country that is located about 1,000 miles (1,600 kilometers) from the U.S. mainland. Puerto Rico is an island in the Caribbean Sea. It lies between the Dominican Republic and the Virgin Islands.

Puerto Rico is a commonwealth of the United States. Puerto Rico is the main island of the territory. The islands of Culebra and Vieques also belong to the territory. These two small islands are located off the east coast of Puerto Rico. The people of Puerto Rico are U.S. citizens. They are mostly of Spanish or African descent. Spanish is the official language spoken here.

The island is split by a central mountain range. El Yunque, the only tropical rainforest in the U.S. National Park system, is located in the northeast part of the island.

The tropical climate, beautiful beaches, sportfishing, and ancient forts are just a few of the tourist attractions.

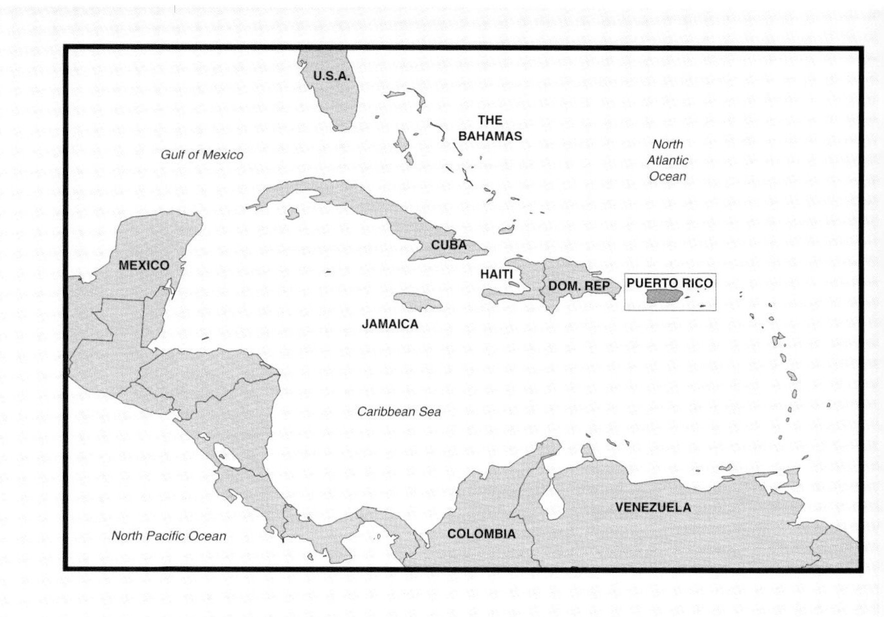

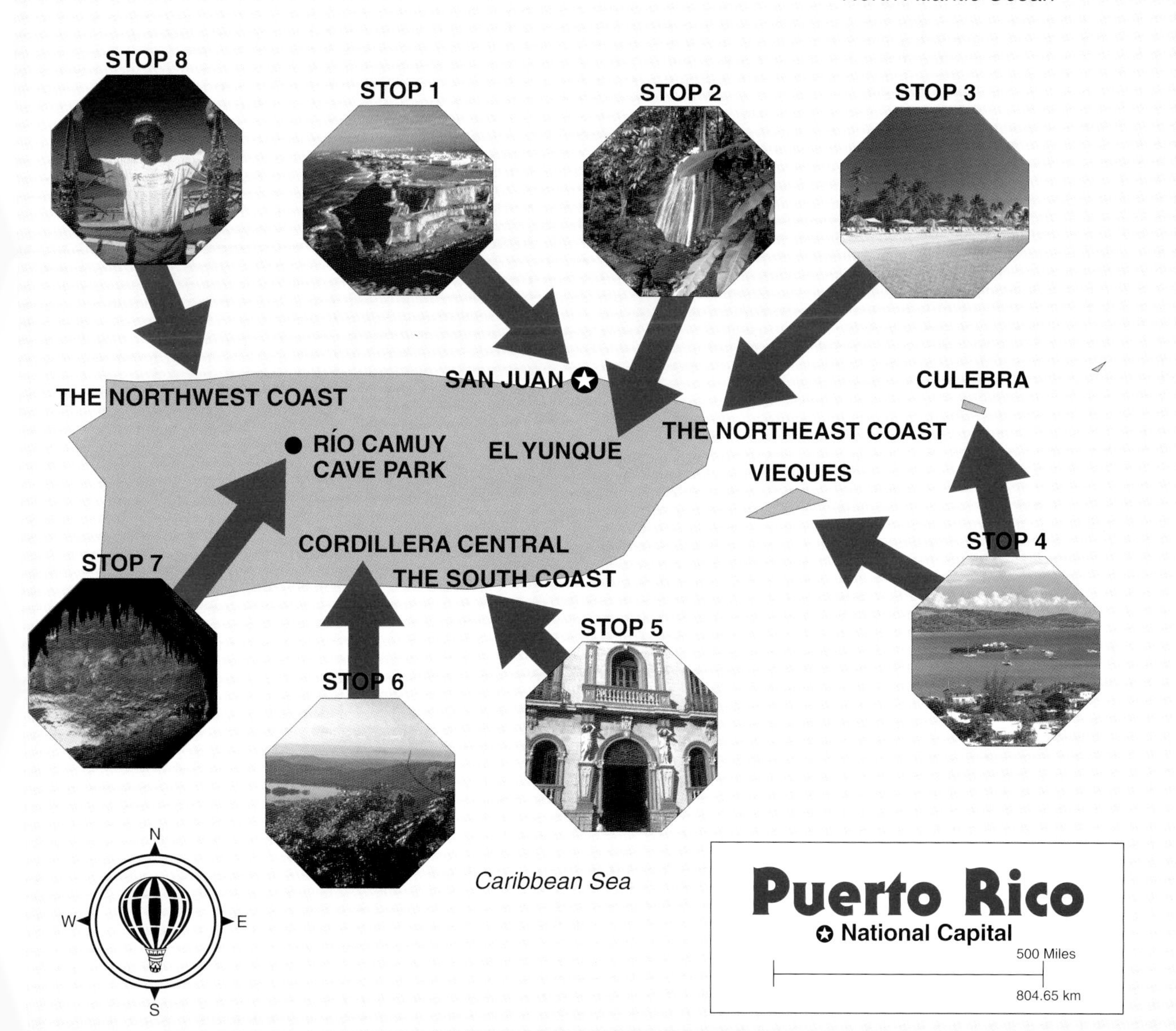

Puerto Rico

National Capital

500 Miles

804.65 km

Stop 1: San Juan

The city of San Juan is located on the eastern end of the north coast of the island. It is the oldest American city. For centuries it was one of the most important harbors in the New World. Today it remains the Caribbean's major port.

The most interesting place to visit here is Old San Juan. This is the original walled city, and the streets are paved with iron bricks. Wandering these narrow streets is like taking a journey through history. There are many historic buildings and homes painted pink, orange, pastel green, and white.

At the entrance to San Juan Bay you will see El Morro. This fort is one of the country's most famous landmarks.

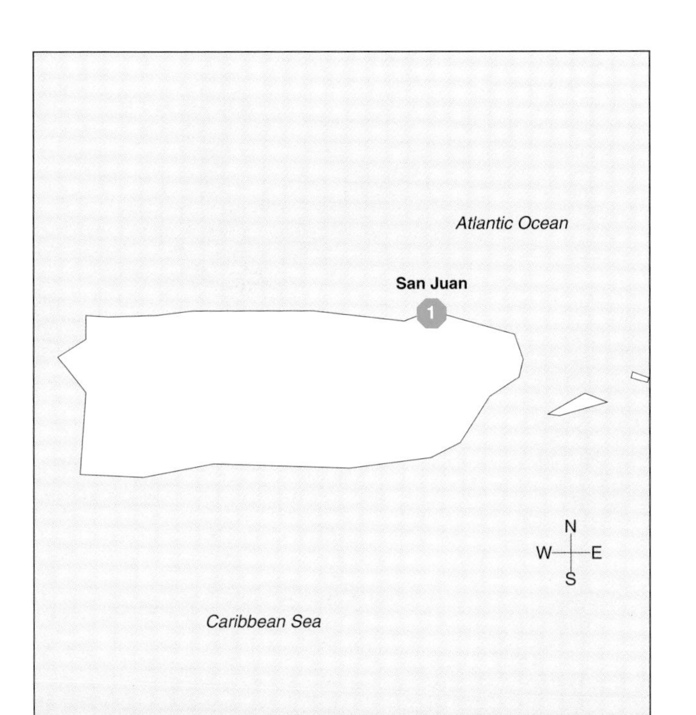

Opposite: El Morro.

Now let's fly ***south-east*** *to El Yunque.*

Stop 2: El Yunque

The Caribbean National Forest, know as El Yunque, is the only tropical forest in the United States National Park system. It is located in the Sierra de Luquillo mountains at the eastern end of the island.

El Yunque has one of the island's most extreme climates. It receives about 240 inches (6 meters) of rain a year!

Here you will find tree frogs, the endangered Puerto Rican parrot, and the Puerto Rican boa. The boa is the island's largest snake and can grow to 7 feet (2 meters) long. El Yunque is a forest of many types. You can see warm, dry forest as well as mossy, tropical forest. It is most famous for its pine forest.

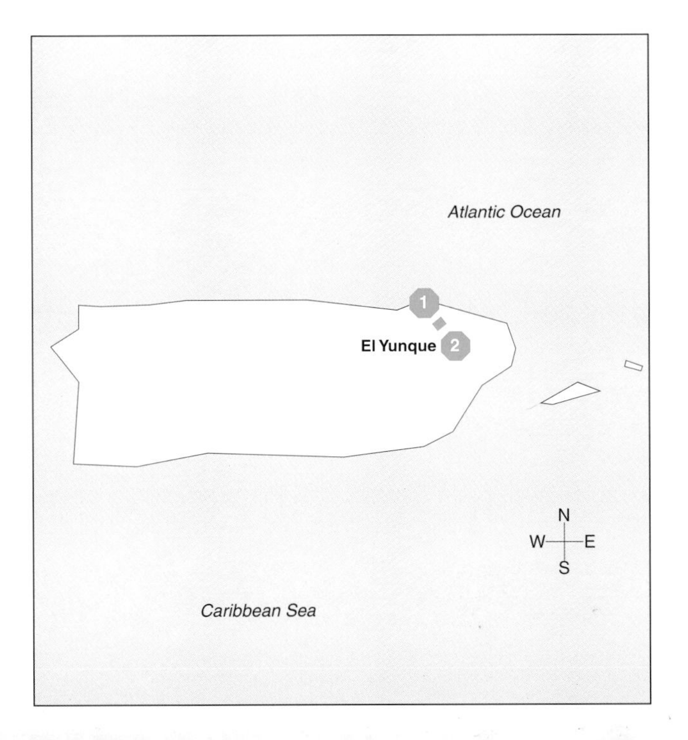

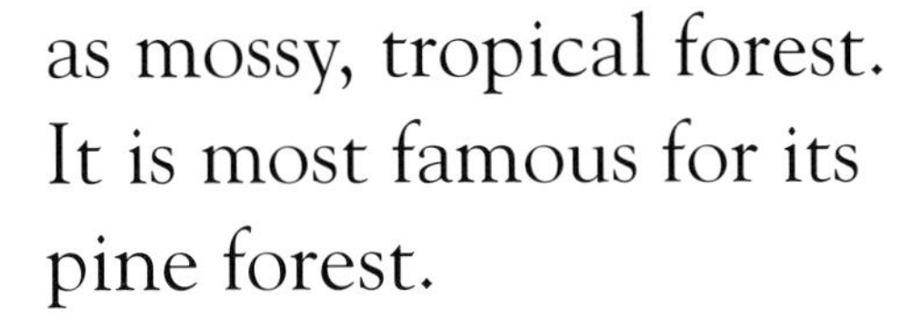

Now let's travel to the ***northeast*** *region of the island.*

Growing Up in Puerto Rico

Puerto Ricans value a good education. Many students go on to college after graduating from high school. Spanish is the language used in the classroom and in daily life. Students are required to take English as a second language in school.

Because Puerto Rico is a territory of the United States, schoolchildren sing "The Star Spangled Banner" before singing their island's anthem.

Families in Puerto Rico are close and supportive. Relatives usually live in the same neighborhood or town, and visit frequently. Grandparents often provide child care when both parents are working.

Children often live at home with their parents until they get married. Many Puerto Ricans marry as early as 16-17-years-old. With increasing emphasis on education, however, more Puerto Ricans are waiting to marry until they are older and have finished school.

Stop 3: The Northeast Coast

The northeastern region of Puerto Rico offers a variety of landscapes and cultures.

Loíza is a world of African culture and ritual. Just a short drive west from San Juan is Luquillo, considered the island's most beautiful beach. From here you can see the peaks of the El Yunque rain forest.

Fajardo is the first major town along the northeast coast. It offers the best sailing in the Caribbean. From here you can take a ferry to the offshore islands of Vieques and Culebra. An important attraction in this region is the neoclassical lighthouse known as El Faro.

Icacos is a cay, or offshore sandbank. The reefs here are abundant with a variety of corals, plant, and animal life.

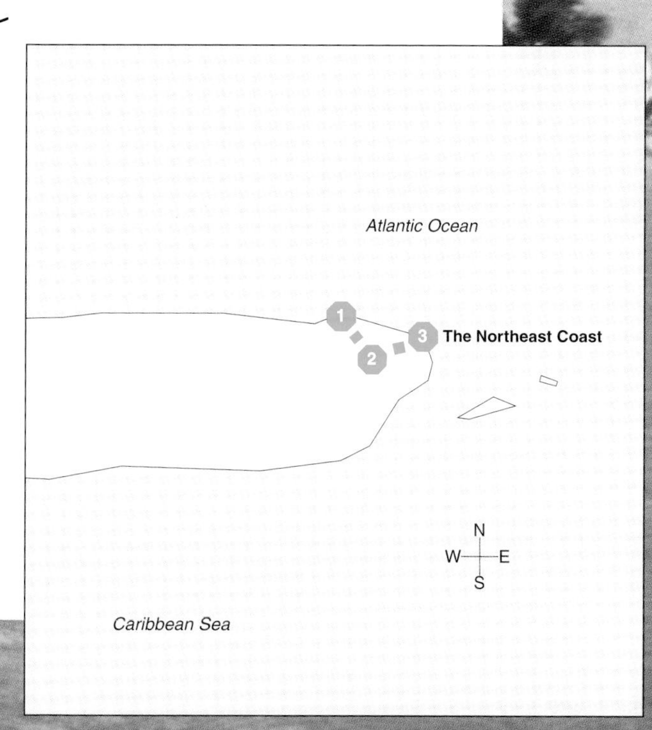

Now let's fly ***south-east*** *to the offshore islands of Vieques and Culebra*

Stop 4: Vieques and Culebra

Six miles off the east coast of Puerto Rico lies the island of Vieques. You can take the ferry from Fajardo to the island. Vieques has a variety of landscapes. You will see dry hills, beaches, a small rain forest, and exotic wildflowers. There are about one hundred beautiful pasofino horses roaming wild on the island.

North of Vieques is the peaceful island of Culebra. There is a subtropical "rock forest" here where exotic Caribbean plants grow amid thousands of large boulders.

The crystal clear waters surrounding both islands make them ideal spots for snorkeling, swimming, and scuba diving. An interesting fact about Culebra is that pirates once used the island as a hiding place.

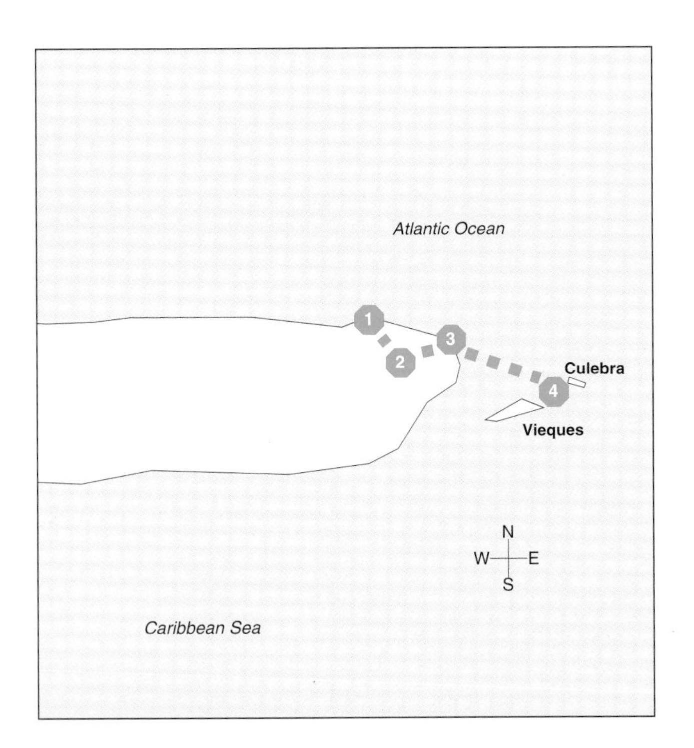

Opposite: Flamenco Beach, Culebra.

Now let's travel to the ***southern*** *coast of the island.*

Stop 5: The South Coast

The southern coast of Puerto Rico has a climate different from anywhere else on the island. It is very dry and almost never rains.

In the southeast region, the Guanica Forest Reserve is home to half of the island's bird species. Here you can see the endangered Puerto Rican whippoorwill.

The city of Ponce is Puerto Rico's second largest city and one of the Caribbean's most beautiful cities. In the southwest region is the city of Parguera. The bay here is famous for it's micro-organisms that "glow in the dark."

The city of Mayagüez is known for its tuna canneries. They supply more than half the tuna eaten in the United States.

***Left:* A house in Ponce.**
***Opposite:* A beach in the Guanica Forest Reserve.**

*Now let's fly **northward** to the Cordillera Central.*

Atlantic Ocean
1
2
3
4
5
The South Coast
N
W
E
S
Caribbean Sea

Stop 6: Cordillera Central

The highest mountain range on the island is the Cordillera Central. These mountains run east-west and are located off-center, closer to the south coast. This is a remote region of peaks and valleys that few visitors explore. Here you will find cool mountain lakes, waterfalls, and streams. Cerro de Punta, the island's highest peak, is the coolest spot on the island. From here you have a spectacular view of San Juan.

The most interesting place to visit in this region is the Caguana Indian Ceremonial Ballpark. The native Taínos built the ballpark nearly a thousand years ago. Here, the ball game they played was a blend of sport and religious ceremony.

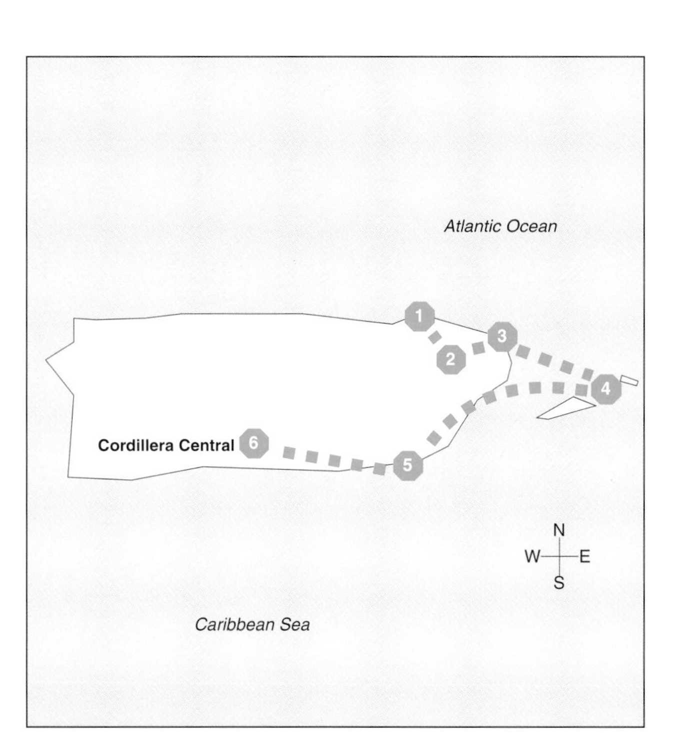

Now let's travel ***northwest*** *to the Río Camuy Cave Park.*

The Cordillera Central.

Stop 7: Río Camuy Cave Park

The Río Camuy Cave Park lies in the north-western region of the island. The subterranean caverns here were carved out by the Camuy River. They are more than one million years old. This park has one of the largest cave networks in the Western Hemisphere.

Hike through a beautiful fern-filled ravine on your way to the opening of the caverns. At the entrance you will see stalactites descending from the bushy hillside.

The native Taínos believed that these formations were sacred. Many of the Taínos artifacts have been found in the caves.

The main attraction here is Clara Cave. It is 170-feet (51 meters) high. The cave has been dramatically lit.

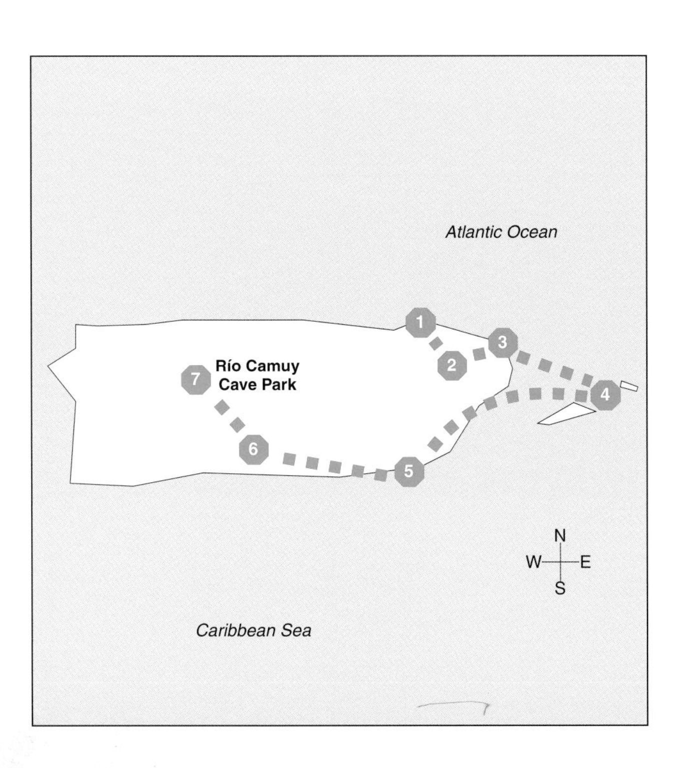

Now let's travel to the ***northwest*** *coast of the island.*

The Foods of Puerto Rico

Puerto Rican cooking is a mixture of native Taíno, Spanish, and African traditions.

The plantain is a basic ingredient in Puerto Rican cuisine. It looks like a large green banana but is actually a vegetable. *Pinon* is a popular dish made with plantains and well-seasoned ground beef. It is served with rice, like most dishes on the island.

The base of many native dishes is the *sofrito*, a tomato sauce that is tasty but not too spicy. *Sofrito* adds a zesty taste to stews, rices, stewed beans, and a variety of other dishes.

Roast suckling pig.

Surrounded by ocean, Puerto Rico has a rich variety of seafood to choose from, but native Puerto Ricans prefer chicken and pork to fish. One of the most popular dinner dishes is *asopao*. It is a thick stew made with chicken, pork, or seafood.

For holidays and large family gatherings, Puerto Ricans look forward to eating roast suckling pig, pigeon peas, and tamales made from plantains. Also reserved for special occasions is a coconut dessert called *majarete*.

Stop 8: The Northwest Coast

The northwest coast of Puerto Rico is most famous for its sinkholes and caves, known as karst. These unique limestone formations are found in only a few places on earth. Much of the karst are covered with pine and mahogany forests and are protected by the government.

Arecibo is one of the island's oldest towns. It is famous for the rum that is produced here.

Visit the Arecibo Ionospheric Observatory to see the most sensitive radio telescope in the world.

At the Río Camuy Cave Park you can see one of the largest cave systems in the Western Hemisphere. The native Taínos considered these formations sacred.

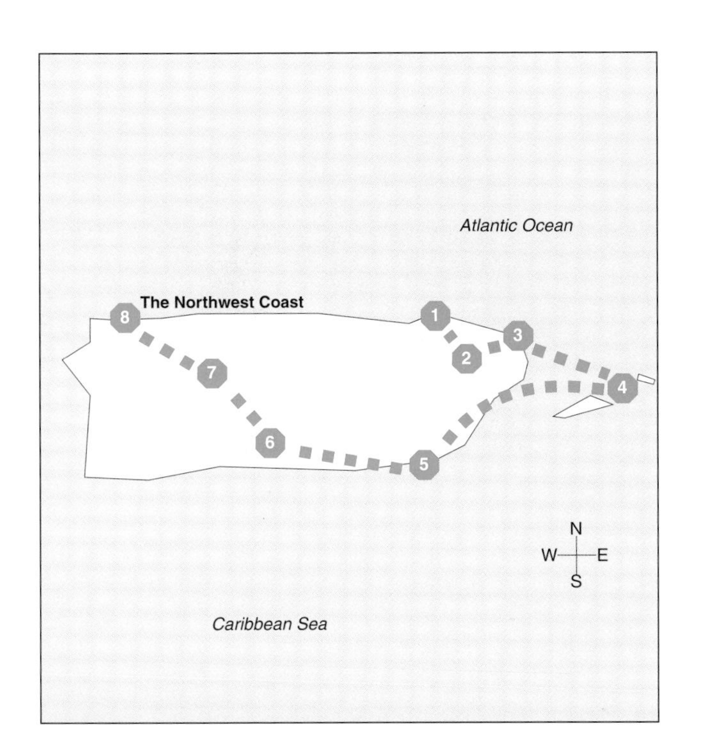

Now it's time to set sail for home.

Coca-Cola
THIS IS
PAPIAMENTO
ARUBA

Glossary

artifacts Any object made by human work. For example, a primitive tool or vessel belonging to an ancient civilization.

cay A low island, coral reef, or sandbank off the mainland.

karst A region made up of limestone that has deep cracks, sinkholes, and underground caverns.

plantain A green, tropical banana eaten as a vegetable.

rain forest A dense, tropical forest that gets heavy rainfall throughout the year.

stalactite An icicle-shaped mineral deposit that hangs from the roof of a cave.

Further Reading

Bell, Brian. *Insight Guides, Puerto Rico.* Houghton Mifflin Company, 1995.

Castello Cortes, Ian. *World Reference Atlas.* New York: Dorling Kindersley Limited, 1995.

Masters, Robert V. *Puerto Rico in Pictures.* New York: Sterling, 1979.

Palmer, John. *Guide to Places of the World.* New York: The Reader's Digest Association, Inc., 1995.

Suggested Web Sites

Britannica Online
<http://www.info@eb.com>

Knowledge Adventure Encyclopedia
<http://www.adventure.com>

Search engine:
<http:www//yahoo.com>

Index

Acknowledgments and Photo Credits
Cover and pp. 11, 13, 15, 16–17, 19, 21, 25, 26, 27, 29: ©Bob Krist/Courtesy Puerto Rico Tourism Company;
pp. 23: ©Joe Colon/Courtesy Puerto Rico Tourism Company.
Maps by Paul Calderon.